The Hungry Wolf

For Viggo and Jethro, enjoy growing up with stories! — L. D.

For Matilda ... Lots of love, Auntie Mels x — M. W.

Barefoot Books
2067 Massachusetts Ave
Cambridge, MA 02140

Series Editor: Gina Nuttall
Text copyright © 2013 by Lari Don
Illustrations copyright © 2013 by Melanie Williamson
The moral rights of Lari Don and Melanie Williamson have been asserted

Graphic design by Penny Lamprell, Hampshire, UK
Color separation by B & P International, Hong Kong
Printed in China on 100% acid-free paper
This book was typeset in Tractor, Classy Diner and Bembo Infant
The illustrations were prepared in acrylic, pencil and chalk

Thank you to Miss Stephen's Class 5, Foxmoor Primary School, Cashes Green, UK
for their help with the speech bubbles

Sources:
Inspired by trickster tales from all over the world, including:
Aardema, Verna. *Borreguita and the Coyote*. Dragonfly Books, New York, 1998.
Matthews, John and Caitlin. *Trick of the Tale*. Templar, Surrey, 2008.
Sherman, Josepha. *Trickster Tales*. August House, Atlanta, 1996.

ISBN 978-1-84686-872-6

Library of Congress Cataloging-in-Publication Data
is available under LCCN 2012020209
1 3 5 7 9 8 6 4 2

The Hungry Wolf

A Story from North America

Retold by Lari Don • Illustrated by Melanie Williamson

Barefoot Books
step inside a story

Contents

CHAPTER 1

The Fluffy White Animal

The young wolf was hungry and hunting for food.

His granny had told him never to eat anything if he did not know its name. It might be dangerous — it might bite back or give him a sore tummy.

The wolf spotted a small animal playing
in the field above the river. It was white and
fluffy, and smelled like a snack. He did not
know its name, so he knew he should not
eat it.

But the wolf was very hungry, so
he came up with a plan.

Yum!

He trotted up to the fluffy animal,
and said, "Good morning! I'm called Wolf.
What are you called?"

The animal gazed up at him with
wide eyes and she said, "I'm very new, and
I don't know what I'm called."

"Come on!" said the wolf. "You
must know what you're called."

"Maybe I don't have a name."

"Everything has a name," said
the wolf.

I don't
know.

The wolf looked around. "This is grass,
and these are flowers," he said. "I'm a wolf,
that's a butterfly. Everything has a name.
You must have a name."

The fluffy animal said, "The farmer painted something on my wool this very morning. Maybe that was my name. Can you read it?"

The wolf walked around the white animal, and saw blue markings on her side. But the blue paint just looked like dots and swirls. "I can't read that," he said.

"You're standing too close to me.
Take another step back to get a better
view. Then you'll read the letters, and
you'll know my name."

The wolf took a step around, and
a step back, to get the best view.

Suddenly, the wolf fell backward off the cliff into the fast river below. As he was swept away, the fluffy animal perched on the cliff top and shouted, "I'm a lamb, I am. I'm a lamb, you silly wolf, and you will never eat me!"

I tricked you!

CHAPTER 2

A Picnic

A few weeks later, the young wolf
made his way back to the field to try to
catch the lamb again. His back hurt, and
he had a nasty cold, but he was sure he
would get her this time.

She was bigger now, but she could not
run as fast as the wolf. So he pounced on
her, grabbed her and carried her away
from the cliff and the river, into the hills.

He stopped to eat her in a rocky
valley. The lamb said, "I know this place.
My uncle Long Horn lives here. If he saw
you eat me here, he would be angry, and
he would prod you with his horns. Maybe
you should eat me somewhere else.'

17

The wolf kept trotting around with
the lamb in his mouth, until he reached a
stony hilltop. He was panting, the hill was
steep, his mouth was full of fluff. Could he
put the lamb down and eat her here?

"I know this place," the lamb told him. "My auntie Sharp Hooves lives here. If she saw you eat me here, she would be annoyed, and she would kick you with her hooves. Maybe you should eat me somewhere else."

The wolf kept walking around with
the lamb in his mouth. At last he reached
a flat piece of rock on the other side of
the hill.

"I know this place," the lamb said. "My brother Big Tooth lives here. If he saw you eat me here, he would be grumpy, and he would bite you with his teeth. Maybe you should eat me somewhere else."

stony
hilltop

flat
rock

rocky
valley

hills

lamb's
field

cliff

river

The wolf gave a long sigh, and kept
limping around with the lamb in his
mouth. Finally, he was so tired, he fell over
and started to snore. The lamb wriggled
out of his jaws and trotted home.

CHAPTER 3

The Wonderful Singer

The next time the wolf caught the
lamb, he held her tight in his jaws. "It's
nighttime now," he mumbled through her
fluffy fleece. "So this time, no one will see
me eat you. I can stop where I like!"

"That's true," said the lamb calmly.
"But you know, I've heard some nice
things about you since we last met."

"I've heard that a wolf sings like no other animal. Larks sing to the sunrise, crickets sing to the sunset, but wolves sing to the moon. And I've heard that you sing better than any other wolf," said the lamb.

The wolf grinned around the wool in his jaws. He had been better at howling than all the other wolf cubs.

"I would love to hear you sing, just once, before I'm eaten," said the lamb. "Please sing for me."

So the wolf put the lamb down, pointed his nose at the moon, and howled. He howled the wolf song to the moon, and he howled loud and long.

When he finished and looked down, the lamb had vanished. In the silence after his song, he could hear her laughing as she trotted home.

You'll never catch me!

CHAPTER 4

A Snack or Dinner?

The wolf caught the lamb again.

"Well done," she said. "You caught me again. But what a shame I'm just a snack, not a meal. I'm still so little. If you eat me now, you'll be hungry again by supper, won't you?"

The wolf nodded.

"But if you wait until I've eaten lovely green grass all summer, then I'll be such a big meal, you could invite your whole family around for dinner."

The wolf could feel the lamb's body
in his mouth, and she was right. She was
mostly fluff, not much meat at all.

"You've always caught me before," said
the lamb. "And I'll be even slower when
I'm a sheep, so I'm sure you'll catch me
again. And I will be a much bigger catch."

The wolf thought about eating a
sheep rather than a lamb. So he put the
lamb down.

"See you soon," she said as she ran off.

Whenever the wolf saw the lamb in the distance that summer, she waved to him. "Look how hard I'm working for you! I'm eating as much as I can, to get nice and fat!"

Eat up!

CHAPTER 5

The Menu

In the autumn, the wolf caught the
lamb again. But now she was a sheep.
She was big and plump and smelled
exactly like supper.

"Well done, you caught me again,"
she said in her lovely soft voice. "I hope I'll
make an excellent dinner. Did you invite
all your friends and family around?"

The wolf nodded.

"Am I going to be a proper meal?" she asked. "With three courses?"

The wolf shook his head.

"Oh. What about some cheese at the end of the meal at least?" asked the sheep.

The wolf shook his head again.

"Oh. I'm a bit offended. I did all
that work over the summer, fattening up
for you, and now you aren't even having
a fancy dinner. I'm a bit hurt."

The sheep went all floppy in his mouth.

The wolf sighed.

Then the sheep said, "I have an idea.
I would feel happier about being eaten if
you had just one bit of cheese afterward.
I know where you can get some cheese."

"Where?" mumbled the wolf.

"In the river," said the sheep. "There's a big, round, white cheese floating in the river. Wade in and hook it out with your claws, then serve up sheep for the main course, and cheese for dessert."

The wolf trotted down the path to the river bank. The sheep was right. There was a big, round, white cheese floating in the water.

Promise me?

He dropped the sheep, and put his
heavy claws on her back. "Last time I put
you down, you ran off. Will you promise to
stay here while I fetch the cheese?"

"I promise I will be right here when
you come out of the river with that
cheese," said the sheep with a smile.

The wolf stepped into the river, and walked slowly toward the cheese. But as he got nearer, the cheese slipped away, farther into the middle of the river. As he paddled through the water, the ripples broke up the cheese. And as he got closer, the current pulled him off his paws.

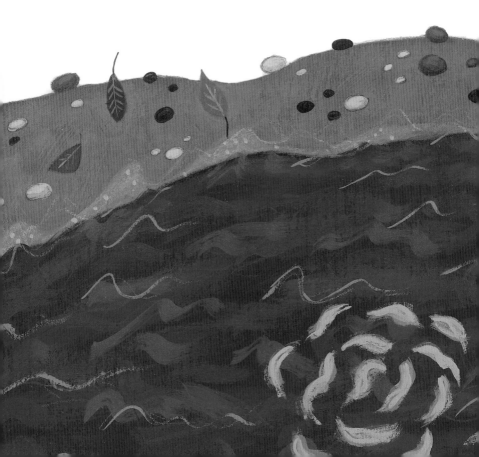

As he splashed and thrashed, trying to
get out of the river, he looked up and saw
the round, white moon shining down at him.

He had been fishing for the moon's
reflection on the water!

As the fast river swept the wolf away, he
heard the sheep laugh again.

Brrr! This
is cold!

CHAPTER 6

Eating the Sheep

When the winter had passed, the wolf
saw the sheep standing in the far corner of
her field again.

He remembered all the times she had
tricked him.

This time, he thought, he would not talk
to her, and he would not let her talk to him.
Not one word.

He would just eat her, right there and then.

So he jumped onto the sheep, sank
his teeth into her woolly fleece and took
a big bite.

Then he howled. "Ow! Her insides are
sharp and hard and salty!" He coughed
and spat. "My tongue is sore! My throat
is burning!" He ran down to the river for
a drink.

But he lost his balance, fell in, and was swept away for the third time. As the water carried him off, he yelled, "That sheep tasted horrible. I will never try to eat sheep or lamb again."

The sheep stepped out from behind
a rock. She looked at the model she had
made from thorny branches, salty clay and
old bits of fleece.

Then she called, "Come out,
my lambs."

Two tiny, fluffy lambs trotted out from behind the rock.

"Clever little lambs have to learn how to talk and think their way out of wolves' mouths," the sheep said.

They could still hear the wolf howling from far away: "I will never try to eat sheep again!"

The sheep smiled. "Come here, my lambs, and let me tell you some more of my clever tricks."

The little lambs cuddled up to their mom. She told them a story which started, "The young wolf was hungry and hunting for food . . ."

Listen closely, my lambs...